Double Creature Feature

This is a work of fiction. Similarities to real people, places, or events are entirely coincidental.

DOUBLE CREATURE FEATURE

First edition. December 1, 2023.

Copyright © 2023 Eady H.

ISBN: 979-8223437147

Written by Eady H.

Table of Contents

Hairball! 1

We are the Fruit 10

Medium Dick 44

We are all either Dolls or Seeds 48

Bury their Bodies Burn their Heads 51

Big Dick the Game Warden vs The Shit Bear 55

The End of Creation Enforcement (Valoryn Universe) 58

This book is dedicated to all of the B list movies with great one liners and soundtracks. The kinds of movies that can turn a day around.

Cover art by Ruth Anna Evans

Illustrations by Aadyn Hughes

Hairball!

A misty rain hung in the air as Kim opened her door to the pizza delivery man and her cat Mittens ran out the door. He was an indoor/outdoor cat, and this was nothing unusual. Mittens scampered to a drainpipe coming out of the hill beside the house. Green liquid oozed out of the pipe into a puddle. Mittens bowed her head to drink, her tongue lapping up the glowing green liquid with the water.

Kim snatched Mittens up. "Bad kitty. That's nasty," she said carrying Mittens back toward the house. Once inside she shut the door and set Mittens on the floor, picked up the pizza box she had set on the hall table and went into the living room where she had paused her show. Kim sank onto the couch, put her feet up and started her movie as she opened the box. Mittens jumped up on the couch next to her and curled up on the cushion. After a moment Mittens started gagging and coughing and a slimy green hairball fell out of her mouth next to Kim on the couch. "Ewww, Mittens."

Kim gagged as she set her pizza down and looked around for a napkin. Not seeing one she gingerly picked up the hairball with two fingers and tried not to gag, again. Carrying it into the bathroom she tossed it in the trashcan before washing her hands. Glowing green slime slid down the drain with the soap.

Kim returned to her pizza and her show, the nasty hairball promptly forgotten. As the night wore on her lids drooped and she fell asleep to the tv. Having dozed off she didn't notice the glow coming from the bathroom trashcan. And because of the tv noise she didn't hear when the trashcan began to rattle and jump or when the hairball exploded through the side of the plastic bin and landed on the bathroom rug.

Mittens, however, jumped off the couch and went into the bathroom hesitantly. She meowed as glowing green tendrils of hair crept across the floor toward her. Mittens approached the ball and batted at it. The snake like tendrils wrapped around Mittens and tightened. The cat's frightened and pain filled scream finally woke Kim who jerked and fell off the couch. Scrambling to her feet she rushed to the bathroom to see Mittens confined in the hair which was tightening until Mittens fell silent.

The pipes in the room began to rattle and groan. Glowing hair shot from the sink and shower drains then wrapped around Kim. She screamed and hair filled her mouth. She gagged as it forced its way down her throat and filled her stomach to bloating before bursting out of her. Kim sagged lifelessly among the strands which joined with the hairball on the floor. Kim's head and Mittens were assimilated into the mass before it crawled from her home.

Tom and Cindy pushed their little girl Becky in her stroller along the dark neighborhood street. It was the only way Becky would go to sleep. Tom felt a snag on one of the wheels and glanced down but saw nothing as they continued to walk. Becky drifted to sleep, and they took her home and placed her in bed. Later, after Tom and Cindy were asleep, Becky woke to a soft glow in her room coming from under her stroller. She crawled from her bed and turned on her light. Hair tendrils reached from under the stroller to inside where it picked up a doll and pulled it under the stroller. After a moment it flung the now hairless doll out into the room. Becky got on her knees and looked under the stroller. Kim's face looked back at her surrounded by writhing hair.

"Hello hair lady," Becky said. "You can come out. I won't hurt you."

Hair tendrils slithered around Becky and inspected her bald head, free of hair from her chemo. The hairball moved away from her as it spied more dolls on the floor and took their hair.

"Are you hungry? I know where you can get lots of hair. Wait here I'll ask mommy and daddy to take us."

Becky ran to her parents' bedroom. "Can you take me to the barbershop. The hair lady is hungry."

"The barber is closed this late. Go back to bed," her mother mumbled as her father snored.

Becky went back to her room. "They said no but give me a minute."

Becky then went to the kitchen and found a pair of scissors before going back to her parents' room and cutting snips of their hair off. She took the cuttings back to her room where the hairball accepted them and added the hair to its growing mass.

"I think I remember where the barbershop is. Come on," Becky said as she picked up the hairball and set it on her head then left her house.

Urgent News Bulletin

Tonight, a little girl walked out of her home after cutting parts of her parents' hair off. She was reportedly talking about a hair lady needing food prior to taking scissors to her parents' hair. Police are urging barbershops to call them if a little girl comes in unattended.

Becky wandered down the street with the hairball resting on her head. She'd been out all night and had not found a barbershop. Now she was getting sleepy but didn't know how to get home. She wandered into a park and curled up on the playset.

"I'm going to sleep hair lady. We'll find the barbershop after."

Becky fell asleep and the hairball rested over her little body. By the time the sun had climbed high in the sky several people had discovered Becky lying in the playset and the hairball was keeping them at bay by whipping out with strands of hair. Becky woke up from their loud exclamations and yawned.

"Excuse me. Does anyone know where the barbershop is? The hair lady is hungry."

"I told you it was her," someone yelled.

"Little girl what is that thing?"

"This is my friend the hair lady," Becky said. "She's hungry. Please help."

"Someone get it off her."

"We need to call the police."

Becky looked around at all the adult faces in confusion. Mommy and daddy always told her if she needed help to ask a grownup, but none of these grownups wanted to help her. She stood to her feet and the hairball kept a perimeter around her as she walked off the playset. The adults kept out of the hairs reach, never attempting to stop her or help.

As Becky walked down the sidewalk, she was headed toward a man wearing a deep V-neck t-shirt. He had bushy hair sticking off his chest and out of the deep V. Hair tendrils shot forth and ripped the hair right off the man's chest. He clutched himself and screamed a girlish scream.

"Sorry sir. She's just hungry," Becky said. "And you seem to have enough hair to share."

Becky ran past the man and kept going on the sidewalk. As she walked, the hairball stretched out and plucked hair from people. Becky plugged her ears from the screaming until she ran into a police officer who held out his hand for her to stop. She halted and withdrew her fingers from her ears.

"Becky?" he asked.

"Yes."

"Your parents are looking for you. They're awfully worried."

Becky's lip began to quiver. "I didn't mean to make them worry. I was just trying to help the hair lady get food."

The hairball slipped from Becky's head and molded itself into the shape of a human then stood beside her. Kim's face staring at the officer.

"What the hell is that?" the officer asked.

"This is the hair lady," Becky said.

"Jesus, I thought the hair lady was your imaginary friend," he said as he reached for his gun.

The humanoid hair shot forth and covered the officer's face. He dropped his gun and ripped at it, but his hands soon went limp, and he sagged to the ground. The hair moved back into the shape of a human and Becky saw he was now bald. The hair stood taller now and looked down at Becky.

"You're not supposed to kill people," Becky told it. "Killing is wrong. I don't want to be your friend anymore."

The humanoid hair turned and walked away.

Urgent News Bulletin

The missing girl has been found next to a police officer's body. The police officer was discovered with all of his hair missing. Onlookers describe a humanoid shape made of hair attacking the officer.

The hairball roamed the streets in the shape of a human, using Kim's head as its own. Her dead vacant eyes staring out at everyone it passed before stripping the hair from their heads. It grew in size and proportion as it moved through the city. Some people tried to stop it by shooting it, but it left them dead and bald on the street. Its feeding frenzy led it to a concert in the park where a hair metal band was performing. It had grown enough it towered over the stage they were on, and it plucked them off with hair tendrils. The hair metal band continued to play as the hair held them to the creatures' back. When the hairball left, the concert goers followed the music like rats after the pied piper.

Urgent News Bulletin

The hair lady as named by the missing girl has now apparently kidnapped an entire hair metal band. It has also been seen collecting hair as it walks down the street. Authorities are urging people who are not bald to stay indoors until they find a way to stop the hair lady.

In the wake of the hair lady, barbers across the city formed a barber's guild that's sole purpose was to feed the monster. They held a barber's convention and barbers from across the country attended. There they heard the good word of the hair lady. Hair is forever. Long live the hair lady.

So enraptured by the hair lady, the barber's guild gave free haircuts to collect food for their god. And when people stopped growing their hair to be cut and began shaving it to avoid an encounter with the hair lady, they began to steal what was left, even travelling to surrounding towns for collection.

One such member of the barber's guild was dragged downtown for questioning.

"What have I done officer?" she asked innocently.

"I've got you on several counts of hair theft," he said.

"Hair theft? Is that a real crime."

"Don't give me any shit you hair cultist," he snapped.

Analise noticed he was bald. His head freshly shaved and sporting a few nicks like he'd done it himself.

"It's not a god, it's a god damned monstrosity. Now, how would one get rid of it?"

"Normal hair removal processes I would suppose. But you're wrong. It is a god. And we are all lucky to be in its presence. But just remember before you go fucking with it. Hair always grows back."

Urgent news Bulletin

Officers have attempted to burn the hair lady as well as given it lice. The hair metal band still attached to its back have recorded a new song entitled 'Oh god it fucking itches.'

A room full of men sat around an oval table. They were brainstorming ways to get rid of the hair. One suggested Nair because his wife used it for her legs. Another suggested hairspray. Now the men were arguing which was better. While the men bickered about products they did not understand, their secretaries tired of fetching coffee and horrified at the thought of being bald left them there to fetch gel and try that. By the end of the day, they had emptied the stores of gel and were approaching the hair lady. Surrounding the hair lady were her disciples the barber's guild.

Analise stepped from the crowd. "None are allowed here unless it is in worship to the hair lady."

"You're fucking weird now let us pass," a secretary yelled.

Analise stepped aside with a sly grin. As the secretaries crossed the line hair strands whipped out and sucked them into the hair lady's mass. They were ejected out the other side bald as the day they were born. While Analise and the others watched over the hair lady, more members of the guild swarmed the city buildings and took over the city. Once there was no one left in the city to oppose them they sent out invites to the hair metal bands concert from the back of the hair lady and invited people from other towns to the show.

People swarmed to the town for the once in a lifetime show. Hair is forever. Long live the hair lady!

LONG LIVE THE HAIR
LADY!

We are the Fruit

6/15/23

Today I saw the fruit of the last ten years of work finally peak their green little heads from the plot of soil that I'd planted them in. God I'm giddy just thinking about it. One stood taller than the rest. A small round pod on a stalk with a pointed leaf on top that looked like a bird's beak, long and slender. I'm not even sure now what I had expected them to look like. And you'd think I'd have had an idea since I had designed the seed this plant had grown from. Even stranger was when I crouched next to my garden to inspect it. The stalk and pod seemed to mimic my movements as my head titled side to side. The beak like leaf opened and closed almost like a mouth and I noticed a slender needle like apparatus inside the leaves. I jumped to my feet excited and yelled for my lab assistant Howard.

When I turned back to the plant, it exploded from the ground and glided toward me. The plant had four more leaves that the dirt had been hiding that looked almost like wings. They wrapped around my right calf and the beak closed on my leg as the needle pierced my skin. I could feel my blood flowing into the needle, almost as if the plant sucked on it. For a moment I was too amazed to move, and I let it feed. It was after all, my purpose to observe my creation.

Howard joined me outside the lab and stood just outside the door. "Kris what the hell is that on your leg?" he asked.

"Our creation," I told him as I started to peel the leaves away from my skin. A sticky substance stretched from my skin to the leaves. I felt the plant shift in my hand, and it used the leaves to slash at my opposite leg and my hands. When I quickly let go of the leaves, they stopped slashing at me and once more wrapped around my leg.

"What's it doing?" Howard asked.

"Protecting its food source. Amazing."

"No, not amazing. We didn't design them to feed on humans."

Howard and I had been manipulating the genes of parasitic plants to make food sources that could grow on other worlds during exploratory missions. Or even one day colonization's. At the very least we might make plants that didn't need earth's dirt to make us food or oxygen.

"What does it feel like?" Howard asked.

"At first it hurt, now it feels almost numb like it might inject a local anesthetic at the same time it feeds."

"We need to run tests on you and the uh . . ."

"Paravamp."

"Paravamp?"

"Like a parasite, but since it drinks blood, Vamp as in vampire."

"Alright let's get you cleaned up and then start running tests on you and the Paravamp."

While Howard bandaged me, I mused on the plants' violent attempts to keep its food source. It was out of character for plant life. Plants were capable of sensory observations in moderation. Taste and touch albeit differently than humans and even animals. They could sense differences in the color and length of light and send signals to each other warning of danger. And they could even use poison as a defense, but this utter violence was completely out of character.

"It's really not safe to leave it on you," he said. "We know it's taking your blood, but we don't know what it could be transmitting to you through there. Like mosquitos do when they are infected with diseases."

"We grew it in this lab where there are no diseases like that. Jesus Howard it's not going to give me malaria."

"I don't like it, Kris. We created something unnatural."

"It's a plant, the very definition of natural. Just imagine if it grows food or an herbal remedy. Think of the lives we'll save. If we remove it, we'll never know."

"I think we should take it to the board. After all it's their money paying for our research."

"I think you mean my research. After all you are my assistant and it's my body so it's my choice. If you don't like it, there's the door."

I was not about to be denied the last ten years of research because he couldn't stomach something new.

Howard sighed. "I just think it's dangerous Kris. We don't know what it's doing to you. I'm not saying kill it simply find a new host."

"What host? We don't experiment on animals here, we're botanists," I said then patted his leg. "I'll be careful, I promise."

I knew Howard was upset and probably hurt by my words. Howard had been invaluable in the lab, and I was grateful to him for being here. But I would not waver in the face of discovery and if he didn't have the stomach for it after all then he should leave. I had meant that, though I didn't want to see him go. This new discovery excited yet scared me. And if he left, who would I have?

6/20/23

Though I have never carried a child of my own, I imagine this situation is not dissimilar. The Paravamp draws its sustenance from my body and though it causes no pain some days it leaves me weaker. I know Howard can tell, but he keeps his thoughts to himself. Ever faithful he picks up my slack and makes sure I eat more than enough to replenish the energy the Paravamp takes from me. I've begun avoiding the mirror because I don't like my pale reflection. I find the sun makes me feel better and have been spending more time outside watching my garden. The rest of the Paravamps have not shown the awareness of the one attached to me, and I worry this one is the only one that will survive. Although if the rest were to suddenly spring from the ground, I'm not sure what I would feed them. One is almost more than I can physically handle, and I know Howard will not consider sharing his body with one. He thinks I do not see the disgusted looks he casts at my green hitchhiker, but I do. A feeling of unease grows in my belly when I am in Howard's presence, and I worry he will do something rash. I hope I am wrong, and Howard's professional curiosity is enough to keep him in check. I cannot fathom his hate for this little creature we created. It is only doing what it must to survive. The very thing we were doing by creating it. My hope is that eventually it bears fruit of some kind and Howard has to choke down his hate to admit we did something good. Hopefully before he turns on the Paravamp.

6/27/23

The Paravamp outgrew my leg and detached briefly only to slide under my shirt and attach to my front. The leaves hug my stomach and chest while the needle has inserted itself into my neck. Its weight is comforting against me. I've lost all interest in running tests on it and am content to just watch it live. Absent mindedly I stroke its leaves under my shirt, and it makes a little trill of a noise I believe is a sound of joy. Howard still looks disgusted by my little friend, and he hadn't spoken to me in a week. Today he finally opened his mouth and I really wish he wouldn't have.

"You disgust me, Kris. You've lost sight of the bigger picture."

"And that is?"

"Why we created that thing."

He spat those words at me, and I felt the Paravamp tighten against my chest almost like a hug. Anger burned through me, and I'm not even sure if it was mine or it belonged to the plant.

"I haven't lost sight of that. I'm learning from it."

Howard had the nerve to roll his eyes at me.

"I haven't Howard. For instance, I know if I eat salads the Paravamp will not drink quite so much from me. Almost like my blood has a different taste when I eat plants as opposed to meat. God, it loves my blood on meat. And one night I drank just to see what would happen."

Howard had no comment because he didn't know any of these things. All he knew was the data he was taught to look for. I was looking outside the box. When I got drunk the plants leaves weren't quite so sticky. Like it too got drunk and forgot to hold onto me.

"And I know that the sunlight I absorb into my skin is better received by the Paravamp than when it takes the sunlight in directly. Because it can't process it. See you've been looking at it all wrong. Treating it normal. And it isn't."

This is where things went south. God, I wish he had just left the day I told him where the door was.

"You're not normal. That thing has corrupted you. And I'm sorry I ever helped you make it. My observations have been sent to the board and now I'm going to finish things."

"What do you mean finish things?"

I wasn't worried about the board. But the look in his eyes scared me. Howard stormed outside and I raced after him. My skin burnt under the leaves and a horrible smell filled my nostrils. Howard stalked toward the garden. My garden full of my children. My creations. They sprung from the dirt and flew at him on leafy wings, their beaks open.

The field of Paravamps swarmed Howard and there was no gentle attachment like my Paravamp had done to me. They dove at him like angry hornets and attacked. They sucked him dry like the vampires they were named after and when he was nothing but a dry corpse, they flew into the surrounding woods and disappeared.

I knew the Paravamp on my chest had warned the others with that horrible smell. And they had protected themselves like mine had done when I tried to remove it. Howard had gotten what he deserved, but part of me was sad that it had come to that. As I stared after my creation, the woods seemed to thicken around me. The road leading out was overgrown and the sky was shut out by thick boughs. Now it was just me and my Paravamp. I stroked its leaves, and it trilled in my ear. Just the two of us now.

Jamie stood on her apartment balcony high above the street, the noise of the city clashing in her ears. The sound made her head spin, and she looked down at the ground. The only thing that could end the constant noise was a sudden fall. She tried not to let her eyes wander to the thick forest that hemmed in the small metropolis. As far as she or anyone else knew, this was the last city on earth. When the trees had thickened and choked out civilization people had crammed into the city. Anything that the forest had swallowed was presumably gone.

Jamie's eyes locked on the trees, and they called to her. An invisible force that pulled her toward the mystery of it. She longed to step just inside to get rid of the noise ringing in her ears. She desired the peace and quiet the trees boasted. Jamie descended to the street and walked toward the forest. People ignored her until she got closer to the wall of trees then they began to stare. They recognized the look in her eyes. None of them said a word, they knew from past experience it would do no good. Those captured by the allure of the forest never heeded warnings. They never stopped on the street and turned around. They simply walked into the forest never to be seen again.

Soon the cracked pavement was replaced by dirt, and she was stepping over exposed roots as she made her way into the dense forest. The noise of the city was almost immediately replaced by silence. God the lack of sound was magnificent. No wonder people never came back from here. The beauty and serenity drew her further into the trees. She could hear her own thoughts again.

The silence slowly filled with the chirping of birds and for the first time since the forest thickened and choked off the city Jamie felt peace. Everything felt better with the noise of the city gone. Her mind was clearer than it had been in some time. A little laugh escaped her as she continued walking.

Within the deep forest she began to see remnants of civilization. Overgrown and crumbling buildings and cars. Her foot crunched something, and she stopped to look down. Weathered bones crumbled under her feet and a human skull leered up at her. Jamie gingerly stepped out of the remains and noticed another in a rusted car.

The euphoria she'd been feeling dissipated, and horror struck her. No one knew what caused the great forest expansion, but they'd known it had cost lives. Here was the proof. The unlucky souls the forest had swallowed. Filled with unease Jamie turned back the way she had come or thought she had come. She hadn't really been paying attention to where she was walking. Nothing looked familiar and she knew she was lost. Unsure what to do, she kept walking as darkness descended. The chirping of birds died with the light and the silence she had enjoyed before now creeped her out.

With her whole-body tense, she trudged on until she encountered a building that stood alone in a clearing. It was bathed in moonlight, and she noticed it had not been compromised by the forest. With no better options she entered the dark structure. In the morning she was determined to find her way back to the city. But now she was afraid to go further into the building, so she curled up just inside the door.

Sleep did not come easy. She found the complete silence of night unsettling and oppressive. She'd never thought she'd miss the overbearing sounds of the city, but they were the lullaby which lulled her to sleep. When morning came her body was stiff and her eyes burned from lack of sleep. Jamie stretched painfully and got to her feet. With the morning light she noticed she was in a lab. The equipment was covered in dust and cobwebs. Her eyes were drawn to a journal sitting on the nearest table. It had less dust than everything else.

With the sudden urge to feel close to someone she opened it and began reading. Disappointment set in after the first couple of pages. It read more like science fiction than someone's thoughts and feelings. It was also filled with illustrations of a creature the notebook called a Paravamp. Still, it was a neat token of her adventure and she tucked it in her pocket. She briefly explored the rest of the lab but found nothing useful to her situation, so she went outside.

Three bare ass naked men stood outside the building with what appeared to be Paravamps attached to their fronts. The creatures were so large they covered their entire front to the top of their legs. Each of them held a spear toward her.

"Oh shit," she said. Paravamps were real. "Actually, really excited to see other people out here. I thought I was alone. Can you tell me how to get out of the forest?"

"You have trod on sacred ground. You'll never leave this forest."

Jamie turned to go but was cut off by three more naked men with spears. Unwilling to risk being skewered she let them bind her and lead her away from the lab. They marched her for what seemed like hours in silence, and she took the time to stare at the Paravamps. They appeared to have a beak like mouth attached to their necks and four large wing-like leaves hugging their upper bodies.

"Does that hurt?" Jamie asked.

"No."

"What is my punishment?" Jamie really hoped they said banishment. She'd never come back. She'd be content in the city and bask in its noise.

The group stroked their Paravamps, and they trilled in response.

"We're going to eat you."

"Come again?" Surely, they had to be kidding. Cannibalism had gone the way of the dodo.

"You're dinner."

"Look we can just go back to my city, and I'll buy you dinner. Call it square."

"No. Only meat will do."

Jamie ran to the left in an attempt to get away from the group and she heard them crashing through the brush after her. God damnit why hadn't she stayed in her apartment. Now fucking cannibals were going to eat her. Her lungs and legs burned but she forced herself to keep going until her foot caught a root and she ate the ground hard. The Paravamp cannibals hauled her up and tied her to a long stick like a pig on a spit.

They carried her between them back to their village. By the time they got there her wrists were chafed and bleeding. The men set her down, cut her from the spit and looped a rope over her neck that they attached to a stick in the ground before tying her hands back up.

Jamie sat and looked around at the villagers who were watching her. There were people of all ages, even children who had Paravamps attached to them. The villagers lived in dirt huts but did not appear overly dirty. All of them seemed to at times absent mindedly rub their Paravamps which trilled in response. Near where Jamie was tied sat a chair made of branches. A woman with the largest Paravamp Jamie had seen yet sat there and stared at her with a thoughtful look in her crazed eyes. When the woman stroked her Paravamp its trill was deeper and almost made Jamie's chest vibrate with it.

The woman approached and cut Jamie free. "Come with me."

Jamie wasn't sure she could trust the woman, but she was quite literally saving her bacon, so she did as she asked. The woman led Jamie from the village, and no one attempted to stop or pursue them which made her think this woman was important to them.

"Who are you?" Jamie asked.

"The creator."

"Funny, you don't look like god."

"Did you hear that Jesus," the woman said as she stroked her Paravamp. "I don't look like god." The woman laughed.

"Where are we going?" Jamie asked.

"I have a friend I want you to meet."

"After that can you show me how to get back to the city?"

"If that's what you wish."

"This friend isn't like those cannibals, are they?"

"She is not a cannibal no."

Jamie breathed a sigh of relief. Why this woman had chosen to save her she didn't know, but she was eternally grateful. Not wanting to annoy her she kept the rest of her questions to herself. Jamie couldn't risk her changing her mind.

The woman stopped beneath a thick tree. "We'll wait here for her."

Jamie looked around the forest. "How long will she be?"

The woman looked up. "Not long."

Jamie looked up and saw a medium sized Paravamp attached to the tree. "What's it doing?" she whispered.

"When they don't have a blood source to feed on, they can get by on tree sap. Remarkable creatures though not what I intended to make."

She stared at the Paravamp which had started to flutter its leaves. "Kris?" Jamie asked. That was the name she had read in that journal.

The Paravamp pushed off the tree and swooped toward Jamie who stepped back. Kris pinned Jamie's arms to her sides and the Paravamp grabbed Jamie in an embrace before sticking its needle in her neck.

"Don't fight her," Kris said. "Don't try to remove her or she will hurt you."

Jamie stood stiff as she felt the leaves flutter against her shirt trying to stick to her. Kris ripped Jamie's shirt off and the Paravamp clung to her skin with a sticky substance secreting from its leaves.

"She's been waiting for you," Kris said as she stroked Jamie's hair. "Please be good to her."

"You promised to take me back to the city," Jamie said. And first thing after getting back she was going to have a doctor remove the Paravamp.

"This way," Kris said.

Jamie followed Kris through the dense forest and felt herself getting weaker with each step.

"You'll need to eat right away," Kris said. "I sure hope you're not a vegetarian because they prefer blood that's been sweetened with meat."

"Kris, I don't think I can make it to town," Jamie said as her head spun. She stumbled and sat down.

Kris stopped and turned around. "You do look peaked which means she's eating too much. She hasn't had blood in a long time." Kris crouched next to Jamie and stroked the Paravamp. "Easy girl. Stop. Things will get easier. She'll learn how much she can take, and you'll be able to communicate with her in your mind." Kris pulled Jamie to her feet and led her a little further. "I can't go with you past here. Walk straight and you'll be there."

Jamie nodded and walked slowly forward. She could hear the sounds of the city barely reaching into the thick forest. Her steps were slow and clumsy and when she stepped onto the pavement her legs buckled. The ground rushed up to meet her. Before Jamie's eyes went black, she smiled. She was the only person to ever return from the woods.

Jamie woke with an uncomfortable weight on her chest and heavy lids. She tried to move but found her limbs sluggish. A metallic rattle filled her ears every time she moved. She turned her head to look, and it rolled like it was out of her control. She blinked several times and noticed a pair of hand cuffs on a bed rail. They rattled when she moved.

Jamie was having trouble remembering where she was, let alone anything else. The smell of sweat filled her nostrils. A trilling noise vibrated against her neck and the weight on top of her shifted and burrowed closer. She felt something sliding across her skin. Large leafy wings rose from her chest then wrapped around her again. Jamie felt her eyes grow in horror and her heart rate sped up. She looked down and saw a plant wrapped around her naked body. It stretched from her neck to just below her hips.

"What the fuck," she mumbled.

A calming presence bloomed in her mind, and she breathed easier. The presence seemed to swallow her mind whole, and Jamie felt foggy and numb. Slowly she scanned the rest of the plain room with her eyes. The only thing that stood out was the IV next to her. She traced the line with her eyes and saw it was attached to her arm. A bag of blood hung from it. Hot humid air pressed against her bare skin. Jamie lay there for several minutes before she felt the air in the room shift.

A man moved to her side wearing a white lab coat. He checked the almost empty blood bag hanging from the IV before looking at Jamie. "Welcome back," he said with a smile that didn't reach his eyes.

"Back?" Jamie didn't remember going anywhere, but then again, she was having trouble remembering anything.

"Yes, you've been sedated for ten years."

"Ten . . . years?" Ten fucking years. She felt the presence in her mind screaming in rage and it set her nerves on fire.

"It was necessary so we could study the parasite attached to you. Can you tell me how you got it? And perhaps more importantly, where?"

Jamie thought for a moment. Everything from before she'd woken up was fuzzy. "I . . . I don't remember."

"That's probably a side effect of the medicine and will wear off. Hopefully sooner than later."

"Why am I restrained?" Jamie didn't really care about remembering. She was much more interested in getting free.

"For everyone's safety," he said.

"Funny, I don't feel very safe." And she was being truthful. A discomfort settled in her stomach that made her skin crawl and her body restless.

He smiled again and it still didn't reach his eyes. "I promise you are."

She knew the promise was hollow and she resented the lie. "When will I be able to leave?"

His smile tightened. "When we've figured out how to safely remove your friend."

Were they friends? The thought of being separated from it pained her, but she couldn't remember how they'd come to be together. "Maybe I could just take it with me." Maybe they were one now. A weird circus freak doomed to be a sideshow for the rest of their natural lives.

He scoffed. "That thing will never leave here."

Jamie felt anger surge through her from the plant and it fluttered its leaves. "It doesn't like when you call it a thing."

"My dear, plants are not sentient like us. They can't feel anger and so it is in fact a thing."

The plants' leaves fluttered again. "You're pissing it off," Jamie said. She could feel its anger as her own. She and the plant had become one at some point. Perhaps before she came to be here. Or perhaps in the years after.

He shrugged. "That's a you problem."

The whole situation seemed to be a her problem. And she wasn't even sure she had anyone to blame but herself. She could, however, make it their problem. "Un fucking believable."

"What's un fucking believable?" he asked as he hung another bag of blood.

"Ten fucking years and you numbskulls still can't separate us. You ever think maybe I was born this way? That I'm a mutant freak?"

He laughed. "I definitely know you weren't born that way. I've seen your birth records. And I know you stepped into the forest like so many others before you, where you differ is that you came back. The only one to every return from the forest and you came back with that."

The word forest triggered a sense of fear in her, but the plant soothed it from her. And she knew the forest was no longer a danger to her. Not so long as she remained joined to the plant.

"It's called a Paravamp. Do you remember that?" he asked.

A part of her did. It remembered reading about them in a dusty old journal. The same journal he pulled out now and held over her.

"Where did you find this?" he asked.

"In a lab."

"Did you read it?"

She thought for a moment. "No? Maybe? At least not all of it." Her memory of before today was still fuzzy and it came in pieces. She thought she remembered reading up till she saw hand drawn pictures of the Paravamp.

"It was very helpful in regard to your friend there. At least how to keep you both alive. The rest we had to figure out on our own." He pressed a button on the bed and raised Jamie to a sitting position then unlocked her wrist from the bed. "The Paravamp knows just how much blood it can take from you before you're too weak to support it. It doesn't want to kill its host."

Jamie remembered stumbling through the forest. She thought she remembered someone with her telling her she needed to eat because the Paravamp hadn't learned how much it could take yet.

"The Paravamp will even heal its host," he said then cut her shoulder. "It's even kept you from falling ill."

"Ow, what the fuck," Jamie said. God, she knew she was swearing too much, but she had ten years to make up for and how else should one respond after waking up like this.

The Paravamp did not move, and the man poked it with a cattle prod. Jamie felt the current course through her own body. Hot rage filled her, and she was unsure if it was hers or the Paravamps. When he released the charge the Paravamp unstuck from her front like it had lost its grip. Jamie caught it and cradled it like a child. In an almost human gesture, it cupped a leaf and touched it tenderly to Jamie's cheek like it was a hand. Then it wiped a leaf across her shoulder and left behind a sticky residue. And in that moment, she knew it to be Eve and their bond complete. Jamie hugged Eve and felt her return her embrace. Before that moment she'd not thought a plant could be sentient or house a soul. Now she did.

"As I was saying that sap will heal your wounds and its antibacterial, so it keeps out infection."

How many times had they done that particular experiment she wondered, as Eve released her hold on Jamie and with precision slit his throat with a leaf. Blood sprayed her in the face.

He grasped at his throat; his face frozen in shock.

"Guess you should have been wearing a Paravamp," Jamie said as he fell to the floor.

She then had the insane thought to eat him which she attributed to Eve. But before she could act on it, liquid nitrogen sprayed from sprinklers on the ceiling. Jamie curled into a ball trying to protect Eve.

I saw Jamie collapse just outside the forest. Her Paravamp had drank too much of her blood. I knew what would happen if I didn't retrieve them. But perhaps it was time for the forest and what was left of humanity to mingle. In preparation I returned to the lab where I'd created the Paravamps. It was time to create again.

My Paravamp, Jesus fluttered against my chest. Absent mindedly I stroked him. He had become an extension of me over the years. Now I hardly recall the time before him.

Jamie sat wrapped in a straight jacket, the Paravamp snug against her. Men stood in a semicircle behind them with cattle prods and a man with a notebook sat across from them.

"Why did you enter the woods?" he asked Jamie.

"Why does anyone?" she asked. Since being frozen she'd remembered what had led to the Paravamp.

"We don't know. Hence the question."

Jamie smirked and might have chuckled if the straight jacket wasn't so tight. She still remembered the pull of the trees. The longing for quiet. "Don't you feel it? She asked. "The desire to be free." Something about the way he looked at her made her think he had before. And perhaps still did. He'd caught the madness. The cabin fever of the city. And he wanted her to cure him. Jamie tilted her face up and closed her eyes. "You feel it don't you?" Eve began to vibrate causing Jamie to hum. "Just give in."

Eve flexed under the straight jacket then began to convulse. Jamie felt her skin get sticky as Eve's leaves excreted sap. The substance stank and Jamie gagged at the smell.

The man fanned his face. "What happened after you entered the forest? What did you see and experience."

"You know forest shit."

"Does that thing attached to you look like forest shit?" he practically spat.

Jamie thought he just wanted to call Eve a thing. "Yes, she does look like forest shit."

"She? How can you tell?"

"Well, I'm not botanist but she told me she's not a thing. Her name is Eve."

"Interesting," he said as he jotted notes.

Jamie noticed the man kept fanning his face and once or twice held his head. She heard a noise behind her that sounded like something hitting the floor followed closely by others. The man with the notebook slumped forward on the table. Slowly Jamie turned around and noticed the guards were all over the floor.

Eve seemed satisfied and Jamie reminded her they were still restrained. Eve removed her needle from Jamie's neck and sliced it through the laces. The jacket fell from around them. Eve reinstated the needle in Jamie's neck and flexed her leaves before wrapping around her once more.

Jamie picked up a cattle prod and key card then let herself and Eve out of the room. Jamie didn't know the layout of the building, but Eve seemed to have an innate knowledge of it. She continued to excrete the horrible smelling goo as she led Jamie through the building. Around every corner seemed to be people lying on the ground. Jamie was unsure if they were dead or unconscious and Eve didn't elaborate. Things were smooth sailing until they stepped into the hall with the exit door.

Men in biohazard masks blocked the door and each one held a cattle prod. Eve slid from Jamie's chest to her back. Jamie sprinted at the men; her own cattle prod held in front of her. She felt little stings in her feet and smelled her own blood. She knew without glancing down the floor must be covered in broken glass. Her steps faltered with the pain, and she stumbled, then fell landing at their feet face down, the men above her. She felt Eve take a giant gulp of her blood before launching off her back, her sharp leaves ripping through the men's suits. Cattle prods dropped to the ground as the men lost their grips and fell into the walls, a bloody pulpy mass. Eve then reattached to Jamie who stood without looking at the carnage. She opened the door and stepped into the city.

Liza woke to the sound of the warning siren stating that the orange fungus had been seen in her neighborhood. It had slowly been creeping across the city. It had first been seen in the neighborhoods closest to the forest. The fungus was somewhat of a conundrum. It grew on buildings, trees, cars, and even people.

Liza worked in a lab devoted to the study of the fungus. Now, she was going to be homeless because of it. The siren meant she had one hour to leave the soon to be quarantined neighborhood. After that, there was no leaving. There was only the fungus. Others had chosen to stay un quarantined neighborhoods. Liza wasn't going to be one of them. She didn't bother to pack. She knew from working the quarantine line that personal items were not allowed through out of fear of fungus spores. It didn't even matter what she wore. Nothing but your flesh and bones were allowed to cross the quarantine line. Liza sat for a moment and looked at the tiny apartment she'd made a home. Now she had to start over.

She dressed lightly then left her apartment. The hall was full of people and baggage. With an exaggerated sigh she skirted through the traffic jam and outside. Streetlights cast a glow over the refugees as they moved deeper into the city toward the quarantine line. She passed a lump in the street with orange fungus growing on top. She gave it a wide berth as the lump moved. She looked away. There was nothing she could do for that person. A dog trotted past with orange fungus growing out of its face. A little girl screamed, reaching toward the dog as her father carried her toward the line, her hands already turning orange.

Liza just shook her head and moved on. She joined the mass of people waiting in line to cross. The guards keeping the peace recognized her and motioned Liza forward. She'd have to decontaminate like everyone else, but at least she got to skip the line. She was just starting to remove her clothes when she heard a motorbike growing louder and turned. People screamed as the driver sped into the crowd. He jumped from the bike, and it fell over sliding toward a group of children with its momentum. Liza could see the fungus on it as it skidded to a stop. The mother of the group strode toward the man and punched him in the face. She started yelling about the children's safety before realizing what she'd done. She held her hand away from her yelling cut it off.

The crowd of people coming across the Quarantine line were naked. Jamie wore a coat to conceal Eve and she knew she stood out, but nearly all of the people around her were terrified and they weren't focused on their surroundings. The guards were all facing the quarantine zone and the people coming through. Eve felt the fear as Jamie moved through the crowd. It slipped inside the coat and whispered across her leaves. The feeling was foreign to her, and these people reeked of it.

For weeks Eve and Jamie had stayed just ahead of the growing quarantine area, but it had essentially cut them off from the forest. And now they were refugees like the people of this city. Even buildings that had once been abandoned were now full of people. There was nowhere for the two of them to go where Eve could be free of the coat. Even feeding was getting risky, but still they trolled the line looking for someone Eve could drink from.

Through Jamie's eyes Eve noticed a woman who didn't seem afraid like the rest. She was calm, detached. Jamie took a step toward her before she felt something jab her in the back.

"Seems you're a bit overdressed," a voice said in Jamie's ear.

"Guess I missed the memo," Jamie said. How she had missed the one guard not watching the quarantine zone was beyond her. Maybe because she was hungry and weak. Or perhaps distracted by the woman who was the only calm refugee.

"Wouldn't happen to be hiding orange fungus under there would ya?"

"Wouldn't really benefit you to find out now would it."

"Open your coat and turn around."

Fuck. Jamie knew opening her coat here among the crowd could be disastrous. She didn't want to end up back in a lab. But she also didn't know if Eve could heal her from a bullet wound. Especially if it injured both of them. "If you say so," Jamie said. She flung open the coat and spun to face him. Eve's leaves flying out and slitting his throat. The man shuddered as blood spurted from his neck and he collapsed.

Jamie slammed her coat closed and ran from the crowded area. She ducked into an alley and slowed to a walk. Hopefully no one had seen what Eve had done.

"Excuse me," a female voice said behind them.

"Fuck," Jamie muttered. "Whatever you think you saw was actually a hallucination brought on by the orange fungus."

The woman laughed. "The orange fungus does not cause hallucinations."

"Through Christ all things are possible." Jamie almost choked on the words. If she'd ever believed in God, she didn't now.

The woman laughed again, this time the sound bitter. "God if he exists has abandoned us."

Jamie turned and saw it was the woman from the quarantine line. "Why did you follow me?" She hadn't even known the woman had seen her.

"I saw a flash of green come out of your coat. What was it?"

It was time for denial. The woman had witnessed Eve kill the guard. 'You've got to be faster,' Jamie berated Eve.

'There's no fucking way she saw me,' Eve said back.

"For your own safety, no you didn't."

"I'm not scared of you."

Jamie smirked. The woman was kind of spunky and cute, but if she knew what Eve was capable of then she would be scared of her. "Lady, I wasn't talking about me."

"Call me Liza."

"I'm Jamie. Now if you know what's good for you, you'll forget you met me."

"Every day I risk my life at work so what's the difference in the threat of death for the sake of curiosity. Now please show me what's in your coat."

Fuck it thought Jamie and Eve. This woman seemed harmless enough and they hadn't genuinely interacted with a person in weeks. Jamie dropped her coat. "This is Eve." Eve fluttered her leaves in greeting.

Liza's hand went to her mouth. "Oh my god. Okay not what I was expecting," Liza said and stepped forward stretching her other hand toward them. "May I?"

Jamie shrugged.

Liza gently ran her fingers over Eve then walked a circle around them taking in all of her. "How did this happen?"

"A trip to the forest."

Liza looked up from Eve to Jamie. "You've been to the forest?" she asked awestruck. "Can you take me?"

"It's not safe for people like you."

"Would I get one of those? What's it like?"

"Like having a second personality," Jamie said as she pulled her coat back on. Sometimes her thoughts and Eve's were indistinguishable. Eve didn't push her will on Jamie too much unless she was hungry. But she only liked Jamie's blood when she had eaten meat. Before the orange fungus it had been easy to pull a person into the shadows and drain a little bit of them, but now that everything was getting so cramped it was harder to go unnoticed while Eve fed.

"Were you a willing participant?"

Jamie had all of her memories back now and she thought back to her and Eve's joining. The plant had not asked her to be a host. She'd simply joined with her. No one had ever asked if she had chosen this. "No. Now not that it hasn't been great reminiscing for you, but we're gonna go."

"Go where? Can I come?"

"Why? So you can turn me in to the government the first chance you get? Been there done that."

"Uh . . . no. I want to study Eve and see if there is any way she can fight the fungus."

"We've been studied. If there was something to find, they'd have found it." For all Eve and Jamie knew the government had made the fungus by studying them and the journal. The orange fungus hadn't shown up until the two of them escaped.

"People are dying. Don't you care?"

"I'm not a person anymore so not really."

"That parasite hasn't changed what you are," Liza said.

"She's not a parasite. We're symbiotic."

"Oh really? What's it given you then?"

"Disease resistance and a personality disorder. See she's a giver."

"The disease resistance could help us fight the fungus," Liza said.

"Then why don't you take your happy ass to the forest where there's a whole colony of these vampiric fuckers and get your own."

"There's more? Can you lead me to them? If you help me, I can get you out of the city because I can assure you that there aren't any underground tunnels that will take you there."

"Who says we want out?"

"I can't imagine keeping Eve hidden is fun, nor easy. Out there you can be free."

"Fine. Under the condition that no one learn of my . . . condition and I'll find you the Paravamps."

Liza smiled. "Meet me at the quarantine line tomorrow at ten am."

At ten am Jamie approached the quarantine line. She didn't figure Liza would show up but there she stood with ten men. Nine of them were dressed as guards, but the tenth looked more studious. Liza smiled as she noticed her weaving through the crowd of people. The Quarantine line was still bustling with people trying to cross. Most of the ones left had visible orange growths. The area itself was chaos.

"Everyone this is my friend, J," Liza said as Jamie joined their group.

"Why the hell is she wearing a coat?" one of the soldiers asked.

"She's allergic to the sun," Liza said.

Jamie just nodded; thankful Liza had no problems lying for her. It didn't make Jamie trust her. After all Liza was using her to find a cure for the orange fungus. The men didn't question it and pushed through the crowd coming across the line. Jamie and Eve breathed a sigh of relief as they took their first steps toward the forest. A place Jamie regretted leaving. How she could have thought the city would help her she didn't know. If only she'd stayed in the forest.

As they walked across the quarantine line and pushed out of the crowd going the other direction, several infected people rushed at them. The soldiers began spraying fire at them. Jamie waited for Liza to say something, but she was silent. Guess it was okay to kill the very people she was trying to save. After her own harsh treatment Jamie wasn't surprised nor did she particularly care. They'd never tried to cure her. At least some of these people might reap the benefits of this trip. Provided it didn't end in failure. The forest had a way of taking from humans. The fire scared them off and soon their group were the only ones around.

"Where'd the fungus come from?" Jamie asked. She'd tried to remain silent, but she had to know. She had to make sure she and Eve were not to blame.

"The forest," Liza said.

"Are you hoping to find its origins out there?"

"I don't care what its origins are. I just want a cure. I want to stop the spread."

If everyone was so certain the fungus came from the forest, then Jamie knew where it had come from. A psychotic scientist who was batshit enough to lure people to a nest of Paravamps and let them be taken over.

Despite being resigned to their partnership Jamie was still a little bitter about their joining. What kind of a dick forced being a plant host on someone. I mean yeah, she'd saved her from cannibalism, but what the fuck. Eve, however, seemed content with Jamie as her host. She knew the creator had chosen her well. She was thankful to be off tree sap and feeding on blood.

"Are we stopping before we get to the forest?" Jamie asked. Eve was dying for some sunlight.

"We're hoping to go straight through. It just depends on how easy the city is to traverse," Liza said.

Jamie didn't figure the city would be too difficult to walk through. She supposed the fungus had killed most of its hosts further out in the city, and the ones that were still alive were easily scared off by fire. The quarantine zone they were in currently proved to be what she had expected. Easy. People with orange fungus stood in windows and doors and stared out at their group. They seemed disinterested in the party. Their eyes were distant and glassy, even the children's. They passed quickly through the area and approached the quarantine line that had been erected prior to the one they had entered through.

There was no one waiting around this quarantine line. A breeze coasted down the street and old newspapers rolled past on the pavement. The scene was eerie as they crossed the line and saw a large swath of orange fungus growing across the nearest buildings. The soldiers immediately pulled masks up over their mouths and noses. Liza and the scholarly man did the same. Jamie closed her eyes and inhaled the putrid air. She smelled something decaying. The soldiers led them further into this older quarantine zone and like the last one people gathered in windows to stare at them. Unlike the others, their eyes were not glassy, they were feral.

"Pick up the pace," the soldier in the lead said.

Jamie looked around at all of them just staring from windows. They seemed to be anticipating something. "Get in the middle of the men," Jamie said as she gave Liza a little push toward the group of soldiers.

Liza and the scholarly looking man moved up among the soldiers and Jamie trailed behind looking around for danger. Infected people came out of buildings up ahead of them and seemed to cut off the street. The soldiers turned down a side street and a few blocks up the same thing happened. Block by block, turn by turn it seemed the infected were corralling them toward a specific location. Eventually they herded them into a dead end that had orange fungus growing up the brick wall. Jamie turned around first, barely inside the dead end and not scared of the infected. She herself had a large growth she covered with a coat.

A wall of fungus infected people stood there hemming them in. One older man, with fungus growing from the left side of his face stepped forward. "You're in the wrong part of town," he said.

"Excuse us, we're headed to the forest," Jamie said.

The man laughed. "The forest is everywhere. Even in us."

"Yeaaahhh, let me tell you I feel that, but we're gonna go," Jamie said.

"I don't think so," he said. "You see, only those of the orange may exist here. And you're not wearing the right color."

"God what is it with all of you fuckers wearing plants thinking you get to control everyone else," Jamie said. "You're not special. You're not the first." She was getting ready to rip open her coat and show them her own specialty when the soldiers swarmed past her shooting flames into the group.

Jamie grabbed Liza and the scholar and pulled them out of the dead end. The three of them ran while the soldiers clashed with the fungus ridden townspeople. Despite his nerdy looks the scholar soon passed Liza and Jamie and they followed him. He led them to the next quarantine line, and they rushed through it. Once on the other side he slowed and so did they. Jamie held her arms around Eve's heavy body and sucked in a lungful of air.

"What now?" he asked.

"We need to wait on the others," Liza said.

"We need to do that off the street," Jamie said. "Who knows how many crazies are in this area of town."

'Who cares what happens to them. They got us this close to the forest,' Eve said in Jamie's mind.

'You don't get it,' Jamie said back. 'She didn't look at me like a science experiment.' Like everyone else had since she'd left the forest. She'd not thought about the human's judgement when she'd been incarcerated, until she'd seen the way Liza had looked at her. With wonder.

Jamie waved the other two after her and started walking. This area of town was the first to be infected. So far, they hadn't seen any people. Jamie wasn't sure if that was because they were dead or because they had moved to the other areas of town as they'd become infected, and the quarantine lines were no longer being monitored.

"Everything is infected. There's nowhere to shelter," the scholar said.

"Then we keep walking until we find somewhere to shelter," Jamie said.

"We can't enter the forest without the soldiers. It isn't safe," he said.

Jamie chuckled. "Because town is so secure."

They walked until the shadow of the forest cast them in its shade and still saw no people or signs of fungus free shelter. This area of town looked familiar to Jamie. She remembered it as the area that had called her toward the forest to begin with. Nestled against the edge of the tree line was one house that looked untouched by the fungus. Jamie approached the door and knocked. Unsurprisingly no one answered and she kicked open the door. No infected rushed toward the noise and the interior was dim.

'I don't feel anything living,' Eve said.

Jamie walked into the gloom. Hesitantly Liza and the scholar followed her. After checking all of the rooms, Jamie sat on the couch.

"I wouldn't," the scholar said.

"Look guy. It's been a long day. I'm tired. I'm gonna sit. Orange spores be damned."

"It's Thomas."

"I don't give a shit," Jamie said leaning her head back and closing her eyes.

'The forest is right there,' Eve said. 'Let's just go.'

"What do we do Liza?" Thomas asked. "They had all of our food."

"We wait Thomas. And pray some of them made it. If not, our mission will be short lived. As will we."

'I was wrong. There is something living in here,' Eve said. 'It's blocked by something.'

With a sigh Jamie got to her feet. If it was spores, she would need to remove them, so the humans weren't turned into plant infested psychos like the rest of them. Eve prodded her toward the kitchen where she opened the fridge. An orange slimy snail-like head shot out of the dark fridge and just barely missed biting Jamie in the leg.

"Ew," she said and slammed the door as it retracted into the fridge. It would be a nice surprise for Thomas when he went hunting for food.

Jamie, Liza, and Thomas waited two days before five soldiers finally emerged from the overgrown city. Two of them seemed to be injured and orange tinged.

"This trip better pan out," the head soldier snapped at Liza as they entered the house.

Thomas immediately took their bags and started looking for food. Eve urged Jamie to start feeding on them.

"I gotta go," Jamie said.

"Oh, fucking great," the lead soldier said. "Go where?"

"Get the fuck out of my face," Jamie said. "If I don't leave, you're all going to fucking die."

Liza held the soldier back as Jamie rushed out of the house and into the woods. She figured Eve needed to see the sun. She wasn't being treated like a plant should.

"What the fuck is her problem?"

Liza didn't know for sure. She supposed stress. They were all under it. "Tomorrow those of us that can need to go into the woods. We need to finish this."

"And what am I supposed to do with them?" he asked, flinging his hand at his injured soldiers.

Liza averted her gaze. "Leave them. They'll only slow us down."

"Are you kidding me?"

Liza looked at him. "No, we need to find a cure, or more than your men will continue to die. Do you want them to lose their shit like the people that infected them?" Liza would not allow her mission to be jeopardized. "They'll be safe here. We haven't seen anyone else these past two days."

He stormed away from her. Even if the soldiers didn't go, Liza had made up her mind. She was entering the forest tomorrow and she was pretty sure Thomas stomach would lead him after her. She heard him scream and a thud from the kitchen and went to investigate. Thomas was sitting on the floor staring in horror at an orange slug-like creature extended from the open fridge. As it slowly retracted, she slammed the fridge door.

In the morning the uninjured soldiers met her and Thomas outside the house. She led them toward the forest, with a confidence she didn't feel. What if this expedition failed and the orange fungus wiped out human life? They walked over vines that stretched from the forest onto the road and toward the city. She felt something snag her ankle and trip her. Liza landed on her back hard, knocking the breath from her lungs. The sky whipped overhead and was soon obscured by trees as she was drug into the forest by her leg. She heard the men yelling and crashing after her.

Suddenly a figure sprang from the bushes and Liza skidded to a stop. The figure turned and she saw Jamie standing over her, Eve wrapping her leaves back around her now naked body. Liza stared up in awe as she took in their joined forms. Liza sat up and saw the severed vine attached to her ankle.

"Thank you," Liza said.

The men burst from the bushes pointing their guns at Jamie. Liza jumped up and stood between them, her hands up. "She saved me."

"What the fuck is that on her chest?" the head soldier snapped. "Has that been there the whole time?"

"It's what we're out here to find," Liza said. "Their disease resistance could help us fight the fungus. I need to study them."

"You could have just studied her. Your expedition has killed my men."

"I need to study them in their habitat as well as attached to a human."

"Fuck you and your plant whore. The two of them disconnect. This expedition is officially over. If you go further, it's without us."

"Fine, good luck curing your men then," Liza said.

"Fuck you bitch," the soldier snapped before leading his men back the way they'd come.

Thomas stayed with Liza and Jamie but looked unsure of his decision.

"You'll need a lab," Jamie said. "Come on." She turned and walked into the forest.

Jamie led them to the lab she had found the first time she'd entered the forest ten years ago. She was hoping to find the creator of the Paravamps, Kris. Unfortunately, the place was empty. It did, however, show signs of use which proved Jamie's theory that Kris had made the orange fungus. There was nothing left to do but take Liza and Thomas to the colony of wild Paravamps like she had promised.

Eve could feel them moving through the forest. There were more now than there had been ten years ago. They were calling her home. Back to the family she'd left when she joined with Jamie. Eve led her host to them and the mother tree they resided in. Liza and Thomas looked up enraptured. The sight of them in the tree was magnificent.

Kris sat beneath the tree absent mindedly stroking her Paravamp, Jesus. She smiled at their approach. "Welcome home."

Two Paravamps swooped down and latched onto Liza and Thomas who struggled to fight them off. They stumbled to their knees as the Paravamps fed greedily. Kris approached and stroked both Paravamps.

"Easy," Kris soothed. "Not too much."

As she spoke, the rest of the Paravamps took flight toward town and she grinned. Through the connection of the Paravamps, Jamie could feel that this had been her plan all along. To make it so humans were accepting of her children. To drive them to a place of need so the Paravamps could live as their biology intended. On blood.

If you enjoyed the double creature feature check out these other titles by Eady H.

Medium Dick

We are all either dolls or seeds

Bury their bodies burn their heads

Big Dick the Game Warden vs The Shit Bear

The End of Creation Enforcement (Valoryn Universe)

Medium Dick

In the beginning there was father god. At least that's what the bible tells us. I don't know, I wasn't there. But what it doesn't tell us is there was also mother. The essence of nature and the universe, she pulled nature from her womb to wrap the strong earth that god had made. Can you imagine that? Ripping nature right out your taint? Then god made a son, Adam. So, mother made a daughter, Lilith.

Maybe it was a pissing contest. Maybe they were bored and lonely. And while Adam was captivated by Lilith's beauty, she had a way with nature and found no interest in him. It was then god made Eve. And for a time, life was good. Then Lucifer took the form of a serpent and moved in. Can you imagine living with a big ass snake in your home? Although this was way before people began to fear them. And since he was an Angel, he was beautiful. Unfathomably so. Lilith found companionship in the serpent, but Eve was also drawn to him and his sly tongue. For no one had asked her if she loved Adam. She was made from him, for him. She'd had no choice. And she was jealous of Lilith in that regard.

So it hadn't been hard for Lucifer to convince Eve to defy god and Adam was powerless to resist her as all straight men are powerless among gorgeous women. What I can't figure out is why they were ashamed of their nakedness. Own that shit. Anyway, God got pissed and threw his creations out. Then he hid the garden from even Mother herself. For centuries, his children have looked for it and romanticized it. Except for one. Meleficent.

Whatever happened to the garden of Eden was a question Meleficent had never asked and if you'd told her by the end of the week, she'd be looking for it she'd have laughed. She didn't much care for God or the devil and was at that very moment cursing them both for giving her life and unnatural gifts. The coupling of the two had led to her current alcohol problems.

Her mouth tasted stale, her teeth were fuzzy, and her head was starting to pound. The bar top was sticky under her face and her arms hung slack at her sides. Late morning sunlight filtered through bent and broken window shades. A nasty headache was snaking behind her left eye, but she was still riding her buzz. She felt mildly okay, but she knew soon she wouldn't. Something was always trying to ruin her buzz. She almost tensed in preparation for it.

Just at that moment, Cindy Galloway poked Meleficent hesitantly in the shoulder. "Excuse me," Cindy said. "Are you the . . . the uh . . . the dick medium?"

Cindy had a problem she believed only Meleficent could help her with. A problem she was loathed to talk about. A rather funny problem if you weren't Cindy.

"It's the medium dick," Meleficent said as she peeled her face off the rough bar and rubbed her cheek. Despite her irritable personality, she had a slim sense of humor. She was sure she'd left half of her skin cells on the gnarled surface.

Meleficent stretched with a yawn and Cindy waved a thin bony hand in front of her face to fan the fumes coming out of Meleficent's mouth. Meleficent had spent the night in the bar and her hygiene had deteriorated with every corpse reviver number two she'd drunk. And it hadn't been great to start with.

"So, you're Melef-"

"Mele will do."

Meleficent hated her name. Once Upon a time her parents had loved it and graced their raven-haired daughter with it after their love of Disney. Sadly, they couldn't spell, and their love of the name had dissipated when they'd discovered what a freak she was. Mele smacked the bar twice with her hand then patted down her front looking for a pack of cigarettes. When she found one, it was empty, and she tossed it on the counter.

The owner and bartender, Dunkirk set a drink in front of Mele. His establishment wasn't even open for several more hours, but most nights he couldn't get Mele to leave. She was a permanent fixture on the end of his bar. He wasn't sure why he continued to serve her. She was mad as a march hare, but he'd inherited her with the bar and his father had always insisted he keep her in absinthe. And while she never paid her substantial tab, she also never got in any fights. Unlike his paying regulars. She'd almost become part of the furnishings.

Mele took a drink and spit. "What the shit is this?"

"A jaded lady. Appropriate, no?" Dunkirk said.

"I'm no lady," Mele said before chucking the glass at his head.

Dunkirk ducked and the cup slammed into the mirror behind the bar shattering it. "You're going to pay for that Mel."

Accustomed to being ignored, Cindy had stood there quietly, but the sense of urgency that had brought her to the bar started to nag at her. "I've got a problem with a ghost."

We are all either Dolls or Seeds

48

I have lived many different lives and been known by many different names. I know a great many things, like don't take candy from strangers. All those warnings seem so distant as I reach out my six-year-old hand and take red licorice from a nice lady I just met. It's been a while since I've had candy.

"I've got a real live doll at home," she says. "Would you like to meet her?"

I nod my head and climb into the back seat of her large black sedan. I like dolls. Most of mine were made from cornstalks. I'd been playing with them next to the road when the lady had stopped. Mother had told me not to. But I was so bored inside. And it was so nice outside. The birds were chirping, and the sun was shining. I was only ever allowed out after dark. And even then, very rarely.

Mother never really let me play outside unless we were with the recycled. But they had become what she called radical. At that time, I didn't understand what that meant. And so, she'd moved us to a quiet town and started a job. I wasn't allowed to attend school, but by that time, school had become meaningless because there were almost no children anymore.

"Is there more candy?" I asked from the backseat.

The nice lady handed me a whole bag of red licorice and I munched happily while I stared out the window at the passing scenery. By the time the bag was empty, the lady was pulling into a long drive. She pulled the car into a garage and shut it off.

"The doll is inside. Come on sweetie," the lady said.

Mother had never let me see a real doll before and I was curious. So, I followed the lady inside her house and up the stairs to a room on the left. She ushered me inside and gestured at the doll staring out the window.

"Jane," the lady said to the doll. "Meet our guest."

The doll turned and looked at me. It's eyes cold and lifeless. There was no soul looking back at me. Even as a child I recognized how wrong that was.

"You girls, get acquainted. I'm going to work on dinner."

"Um, my mom's going to be back from work soon. I should probably get back."

"You live here now honey."

The lady left me alone with the doll. I was a bit confused by her words, but I was still enthralled with the doll, despite how creepy it was.

"Hi, I'm Cleo. Do you want to play?"

The doll ignored me and went back to looking out the window. I sat down and played with the toys in the room. I had heard dolls were bland. Some even labeled them as creepy. Having met this one, I found it boring. Several times I tried to get it to play with me, but it just stared out the window.

Its mother came to fetch us when dinner was ready, and it followed her prompts to leave the room. Silently it ate dinner. After all the candy I had eaten I found I wasn't hungry.

"You'll have to tell me some of your favorites dear so I can cook for you," the nice lady said.

"What do I call you?" I asked abruptly. She had never introduced herself to me and I was suddenly struck by the issue that I didn't know her.

"Mother."

"But I have one of those."

"I'm your mother now dear. And while we're discussing such things, I have some rules I'd like you to follow. No going outside. I don't want anyone to know you're here."

"Why?"

"Some horrible person might run off with you."

I was not happy with the issuance of rules. My own mother had had the same rule. Look how that had turned out. That night I was given a bed with my own room. It was painted light purple and had fairies on the wall. It was more than I had had in a long time. Nights spent in the camp of the recycled were spent smashed into a large common room on sleeping bags while the rest of the camp was being built. Nights with my mother had been spent in the same bed as her. She was so scared someone would steal me in my sleep and she wouldn't hear it.

And so, my days went like this for several weeks. Every day I asked about my mother. Every day that was greeted with this lady was now my mother. I was cautioned to never leave the house and urged to play with the doll. The more it stared, the more I found it creepy. It wasn't like a hard plastic doll. It looked real. Until one day I was fed up with that house. And I left. I had no idea where I was going or how to return to my mother, but I started walking down the drive. I didn't get very far when I heard the car racing after me. It screeched to a halt beside me, and the lady jumped from it, her eyes blazing and her chest heaving. I could tell she wanted to hit me for acting out. But she didn't.

"Get in the car," she said.

"No. I'm going home."

"You are home."

I turned and fled from her. I could hear her running after me as I turned into the trees that lined the drive. I was soon lost and stumbling, and she sounded like she was right behind me.

"Please come back. Please."

Bury their Bodies Burn their Heads

There was blood on my hands, so I knew it had happened again. It also meant I was home. My bed creaks under me, dust coating my sweaty skin. I force myself to go outside and stand at the fresh graves. I liked Liza and Alice and I was glad they'd come home with me.

"Momma, you promised you weren't going to do this anymore," my daughter says as she stands next to me.

"I know Ruthie, but I had to save them," I say. There is no remorse in my voice. I'd done what I thought was right.

"Pappa won't like it."

"Your pappa hasn't been the same since he got bit."

"You should clean up the blood before he gets up."

Ruthie hadn't aged a day since I'd been away, and I'd tried to stay away. I had promised Stanley. She was right. He was going to be angry. "Go to your space Ruth." If there is anything I fear it is Stanley when he's angry.

My ten-year-old skips through the overgrown field and disappears. I go back to the kitchen to mop up the linoleum. I am almost done when I hear the screen door bang and Stanley's boots on the hardwood.

"Claire," his voice thunders down the hall.

I stand and shake my hands off. "In here Stanley."

His bulky frame blocks any possible escape when he enters the kitchen. "Is that blood?"

"I don't want to fight Stan." I'm so tired and I don't have the energy for it.

"Is it blood?"

"Yes okay," I say as I drop the mop and cover my face. "I did it again and I know I promised but I couldn't help myself. I had to save them."

"Get out. I told you I don't want this around Ruth."

I sink into a chair. "Where am I supposed to go Stan?"

"I don't care. Anywhere but here."

"She's, my daughter. You can't keep her from me."

"You did this to yourself Claire. You knew the price for coming back."

I don't try to fight him; I just lift my shirt.

"How many?" he asks.

"Two."

"Their names?"

"Liza and Alice."

He always insists on knowing their names. Perhaps he's trying to make me remember they were people. But he didn't see what I saw. They were still people. They stood watching us now. Stanley takes a paring knife and makes two short shallow slices in my abdomen next to the others. I'd lost count of the souls I'd saved and his punishment for what he considered my misdeeds. But the marks kept the tally.

"Get out before Ruth comes back," he says before leaving the house.

I don't even feel the marks he gives me anymore. He's marked me so many times my brain doesn't register it. My bag is by the front door with the blood-spattered ax I use. I sling it over my shoulder, grab the ax, and start down the grass choked driveway. I don't turn around because if I see Ruthie, I won't be strong enough to leave and I am smart enough to fear Stanley. Flies buzz my face in the heat. I hate the road, Stan knows that. It's why he sends me away and why I never go far.

"Mamma."

"Ruthie, your pappa will kill me if you don't get your buns back to your plot of dirt."

"I'm bored here mamma."

"Off this farm, the world is dangerous. I don't need to be worried about you."

"The dead come to the farm too."

"But you're safe in your dirt. I made sure of that," I say swatting at the fly. "Please go home my sweet."

"No. Maybe I can help stop you."

I hang my head. I don't want my daughter to think less of me, but her pappa has convinced her I'm doing something wrong. "I save people. Like I saved you. Like I saved your pappa."

"Well then maybe I can help."

I pinch the bridge of my nose and sigh. "Please Ruthie."

"Mamma, don't you miss me?"

"I do Ruth. You have no idea how much. But you can't come. Your pappa will take it out on me."

"What if he never finds us?"

The truth was, I wanted Ruthie to come. I missed her terribly. But that ache in my chest could never go away. And so, I ignore her, as rude as it is. She stops talking, but she doesn't go away and we walk side by side in silence. I'm no good at telling time since the world crumbled but I'm going to judge that two hours had passed on that hot road when I hear a daisy pusher. The groans echo through the trees and bird's scatter.

"Ruthie," My voice is a mere whisper as I look around the deserted road, but she's gone. The daisy pushers don't scare me. If I am quiet and can hide then they won't bother me. But I'm curious so I follow the sounds. I find it plodding through a briar patch oblivious to the pricks. This is what I'd saved Ruthie and Stanley from. No longer bound to their bodies, the daisy pushers can't sense them like I can. And therefore, they are safe. I watch the daisy pusher for some time. Neither dead nor alive, it only responds to hunger. I'd heard someone use the word reactionary in conversation once. And I suppose that's what the daisy pushers are. Their eyesight is poor and somehow, despite the dead status they've been given, their hearing is fair to middling. The "dead" rising is like a page out of my mamma's bible come to life. But because they are neither dead nor living, I reckon they are souls trapped in their bodies by the mark of the beast. A man who worked with Stanley had received his from his harlot wife and had in turn given one to my dear Stan. But I cheated the devil out of his soul by liberating it before he became locked in his body. Now my husband can roam the earth, but for some reason Stan chooses to stay at the farm. Screams shatter the stillness and the daisy pusher changes direction. I run to get ahead of him. Branches snap as I push through the woods, but the screams are louder than any noise I'm making.

Big Dick the Game Warden vs The Shit Bear

Big Dick the game warden pulls up to the curb across from a one-story house surrounded by yellow police tape. He sticks a wad of dip in his mouth before stepping from the truck and heading toward the house. He ducks under the tape and enters the residence. Muffled voices lead him down the hall to a bedroom. Forensics is there photographing the dead body of a woman. She is wrapped in toilet paper like a mummy. Four canopic jars are placed around the bed. Three detectives are at the foot of the bed watching forensics.

"The jars are empty," Big Dick says.

All three detectives turn to look at him. He revels in their bewilderment. Not only do they have no idea what happened in this odd crime scene he just got the drop on them. Big Dick on the other hand knows exactly what happened here and he likes having the upper hand. The corners of his mouth twitch under his mustache but he refuses to let a smile cross his face.

"Who the fuck are you and why are you in my crime scene?" one detective says.

"The name's Big Dick the game warden and this is my case now boys," he says before spitting into an empty bottle in his hand. He'd been following the sick son of a bitch who did this for some time. Morgues were full of bodies just like hers.

"Since when does the game warden investigate murders?" the second detective asks. "Since an animal murdered her."

Although some would argue anyone capable of murder was an animal. This murderer actually was an animal.

"This was no animal attack."

"It most certainly was. A cartoon bear did it," Big Dick says.

The three detectives laugh. Big Dick stares at them as he spits again. He was used to being laughed at. Even his partner Ranger Rick had laughed at him when he'd told him his theory, but bodies were stacking up and this was no regular murderer.

"Be sure the coroner checks her ass for flecks of cheap toilet paper," Big Dick says.

"What makes you think he'll find that?" the third detective asks.

"That's how he chooses his victims."

"That's bullshit," the first detective says.

"No that's bear shit," Big Dick says.

Detective two puts on a glove and checks the jars. "They're empty."

"Where are her organs?" the first detective asks.

"Maybe he's taking them home for dinner," Big Dick says.

"That's fucked up."

"Shouldn't you be looking in the woods if it's a bear as you say?" detective one asks.

Big Dick spits again. "No, the sewer, because he's a shit bear." Big Dick walks into the adjoining bathroom and looks into the toilet. "I'm coming for you shit bear." Big Dick spits into the toilet and flushes. The toilet gurgles but doesn't empty. The brown mixes with the water. Bright light erupts from the toilet spraying water and tobacco juice as the Charmin bear flies out of the bowl and knocks Big Dick backward into the shower. He slams his head and blacks out. When he wakes up, he's lying in a hospital bed and the three detectives are standing in his room.

"What the fuck happened?" Big Dick asks.

"Your shit bear exploded out of the toilet and knocked you out. After that he ran through the house and disappeared down the nearest storm drain." The first detective says.

"Did you follow him?" Big Dick asks.

"No. we called an ambulance for you."

Big Dick sits up and starts ripping electrodes off of himself. "Let's go." He can't believe he'd been so close to his quarry and these incompetent fucks had let him go.

"You haven't been released," the first detective says.

"I'm a big boy and I'm releasing myself. The shit bear won't wait." The three detectives follow Big Dick out of the hospital room. "Where the hell is my shirt?" he asks as he rips off the hospital gown. One of the detective's hands him his shirt and he puts it on as he heads down the hall.

"Sir you have to wait for the Dr. to release you," a nurse says as she tries to block him.

"Hang the Dr. I've never needed one in my life," he says as he holds out his hand. One of the detectives places his hat in it and he sets it gingerly on his bandaged head. "Where the hell is your car?"

The detectives lead him to a car in the lot and drive him back to the crime scene. He goes to the nearest storm drain and looks in. Darkness glares back at him. "I'm coming for you shit bear!" Big Dick yells into the sewer.

"Where did the shit bear come from?" a detective asks.

The End of Creation Enforcement
(Valoryn Universe)

Emily pulled the locked door shut behind her before she stepped off the closed porch into the already-sweltering heat of the morning sun. The angry glare of Earth's primary star coated her in sweat in seconds, her clothes sticking to her. Just a typical spring day in Indiana. A searing breeze slid across her moist skin lifting her short hair from her neck, but it did nothing to cool her.

"Morning." The greeting came from the end of the walk, no more than ten feet from her, but it should have been hundreds of miles.

Several emotions warred in the back of her mind at the sound of his voice. Soldiers surrounded her. Unusual for her not to have noticed them. She was getting rusty. Resentment tempered the observation, and it was directed at him, Colonel Edward Jaxon.

"We need you back."

How convenient. A year cancer free and now she was usable again.

She brushed her shaggy brown hair out of her eyes, the wind blowing it right back. "You know I can't. The radiation. . . " She gripped the shoulder strap of her bag. "Besides, I need to be at work in ten. Civilian life problems." There was no way in hell she was going back to that underwater coffin.

"It's taken care of. Consider your next round of chemotherapy on us."

"Gee thanks, Colonel. But maybe you're not hearing me. We're short-staffed and my boss—"

"It's taken care." His hands settled on his hips. "So, stop being an ass."

She wasn't going to give in easy after the way he'd let her go. Pride urged her to refuse flat out but she ignored the compulsion. Emily hated the colonel, even more than she hated her current civilian job, but this might be her one shot to get back into the field. The disappearance of Lieutenant Colonel John Clutch had made her a pariah.

"I think you deserve it for the way you ended my affiliation with you and the others when you discovered what a traitorous wretch my body was." She took a step forward.

He should have let her die. It would have been more merciful.

"Clayton never forgave me but Sam, the twins, Jack, and even Dean did eventually."

"And that means I have to?" Her termination had hurt worse than the cancer. Emily hadn't let them see the tears when the colonel had ordered them to leave her in that hospital. She wouldn't allow them to see her weak. Had they seen what a wreck she'd turned into, they probably would have never forgiven him.

"Whether you forgive me or not, you are coming back with me."

The men moved to take her things. Her bag disappeared from her shoulder and her keys were liberated from her hand. A young officer moved to take her travel cup and breakfast.

"Don't touch my bacon." She warned through clenched teeth. Her hand moved to the knife hidden under her shirt, ready for a fight.

The young soldier hesitated. "Sir?"

"Don't touch her bag of bacon, Lieutenant, unless you want to lose that hand."

"Yes, sir." The young man backed away.

"It pleases me to see you haven't lost your edge."

"I live to please," she said, sarcasm oozing from her.

"Let's go for a drive." Jaxon climbed into the back of the black SUV waiting in her drive.

The open door beckoned to her.

Indecision filled her.

If she got in the car, there was no doubt her life would change, just like the first time he'd invited her to take a ride with him. On the other hand, she hated her cover job, despite its part-time status. Customers were whiny bastards. Emily slid into the backseat next to him and the door thumped shut. The AC welcomed her into the vehicle and she melted into the cool leather of her seat.

"How are things?" he said as the car backed out of the gravel driveway.

"They're whatevs." Emily munched on her bacon. "You know I love working a part time job I hate. Makes me feel normal. Civilian."

Emily hated lying, but she was not above sarcasm. Her life was asinine when she pretended to be normal. Her caustic voice reflected her disgust with her situation and his attempt at small talk.

"You're friends with an assassin. How normal could it be?"

"Alejandro? He tried to kill me."

"More normal than I gave it credit for. But then again, running a cockfighting ring makes for some excitement."

"I gave that up." She fiddled with the seat belt she was neglecting, pulling it out then letting go. She'd given up cockfighting when she'd gotten a contract from Lieutenant Colonel John Clutch. It had sparked a series of bad decisions that had her sitting in this car with Colonel Jaxon.

He smiled. "You can return to your sucky normal life as soon as I'm done with you."

She didn't let herself dwell on the truth of those words.

"Would you at least do me the courtesy of dispensing with the small talk? Why do you need me?"

"Egress One."

Her last post pre-cancer and probably the reason she'd gotten sick in the first place.

"You're aware I'm not a scientist, right?"

"The panel has chosen thirty men to accompany you."

"Thirty men to accompany me where? Did you lose the base?"

"Into the gate."

"Where are my comrades?"

He hesitated. "Already inside the gate."

"You better shoot straight with me, Colonel. If my men are in the gate, why do I need the thirty?"

"The last two years haven't changed you. That's good."

"Why would they?"

"You've been through a lot."

"It's just cancer. Now, what happened to my men?" While she had never been their commanding officer, she had always thought of them as hers. Until Colonel Jaxon had stripped that life from her. Because of that vulnerability, she'd said yes to John. Lieutenant Colonel John Clutch had taken a chance on Emily and had given her a contract while she was recovering from cancer. And then he'd ruined her life, worse than cancer ever had.

"I don't know. We lost contact. Which brings me back to the thirty men."

"I don't want them." She squinted away from the glare coming through the window behind his head. Creation Enforcement wasn't for everyone, and untrained men on an assignment of that magnitude could get her killed.

"Well, I tried explaining that."

"I just need two men."

"I presume their files aren't in the stack on my desk."

The smile she couldn't stop hid a hint of malice. "Of course not. I imagine you already know about my new team." Despite being relieved of duty, she'd created a new team, one that wasn't strictly bound by the government. A team comprised of the only men she could trust. Her brothers.

"Indeed."

"Those thirty men have never seen what we could encounter in Egress One. And I don't have time to coddle grown men. What was it you said to me once? I need men with imagination."

When he smiled, resentment ate at her. She'd surrendered a lot easier than she'd intended to. The small space around her seemed to shrink.

"They're en route. Need anything else?"

The colonel had always been able to anticipate the needs of his men. "Lots of weapons. To be honest, I'm glad to be back."

"What happened to Lieutenant Colonel John Clutch?"

She looked out the window and focused on the woods whipping by the car, the browns and greens blurring together. "I don't know." She knew what had happened to his dead body. It had been left for her, by Dominick Kain she presumed, as an apology for his betrayal in Terrillo. Her brothers had helped her bury him, and they'd never spoken of it again. That had been a year ago.

"Emil—"

"Have you ever met him, Colonel?"

"Once. He asked me what I thought of you."

"Then it's a wonder I got the job."

"I told him you were the best agent I ever had the privilege to have had a hand in training. I assume that's why he hired you."

"I hope the self-serving bastard is burning in hell." Emily looked back at Jaxon. He couldn't possibly have known what he was setting her up for when he'd recommended her to John. Part of her wanted to hold it against him, mainly because she still held onto her anger at the way he'd dismissed her. It wasn't fair to Jaxon. He had tried to help her.

"I've heard stories of his cruelty."

"Cruelty?" Emily gave a bitter laugh. "Cruelty I can handle." She shook her head. "Whatever he got, he deserved." Part of her wished she had been the one to end him. She'd let him manipulate her into a contract he would have never let her out of.

"If I had known—"

"You'd what? Not have told him how talented I was? I did things for that man I may very well burn in hell for." Emily had terrorized the town of Terrillo because she'd thought someone there had kidnapped her brothers. She'd butchered and eaten aliens, like Dominick had showed her. All to find out John had them, and Dom knew.